William Gerard Don, Alexander Fairweather

Memorandum Regarding the Fairweathers of Menmuir Parish

Forfarshire, and others of the surname

William Gerard Don, Alexander Fairweather

Memorandum Regarding the Fairweathers of Menmuir Parish
Forfarshire, and others of the surname

ISBN/EAN: 9783337343538

Printed in Europe, USA, Canada, Australia, Japan

Cover: Foto ©Andreas Hilbeck / pixelio.de

More available books at **www.hansebooks.com**

MEMORANDUM

REGARDING THE

FAIRWEATHER'S

OF

MENMUIR PARISH, FORFARSHIRE,

AND

OTHERS OF THE SURNAME,

BY

ALEXANDER FAIRWEATHER.

EDITED,

WITH NOTES, ADDITIONS AND CORRECTIONS,

BY

WILLIAM GERARD DON, M.D.

PRINTED FOR PRIVATE CIRCULATION.

LONDON :
DUNBAR & Co., 31, MARYLEBONE LANE, W.

1898.

CONTENTS.

APPENDICES.

INTRODUCTORY.

ALEXANDER FAIRWEATHER, at one time Merchant in Kirriemuir, afterwards resident at Newport, Dundee, about the year 1874, wrote this Memorandum, or History; to which he proudly affixed the following lines:—

> " Our name and ancestry renowned or no,
>
> Free from dishonour, 'tis our pride to show."

As his memorandum exists only in manuscript, and so might easily be lost, I proprose to re-edit it for printing; with such notes, and corrections as I can furnish.

Mr. Fairweather had sound literary tastes, and was a keen archæologist and genealogist; upon which subjects he brought to bear a considerable amount of critical acumen.

The deep interest he took in everything connected with his family and surname naturally endeared him to all his kin; while, unfailing geniality and lively intelligence, made him a wide circle of attached friends.

I only met him once, when he visited Jersey in 1876; where I happened to be quartered, with the Royal Artillery, and where he sought me out.

I can recall a hale, kindly bachelor, of over sixty; who, having put business aside was then in the enjoyment of a well-earned competency. Yet at that very time, a great, but unsuspected and unforeseen calamity menaced his fortune; for, being an unlimited Shareholder in the City of Glasgow Bank, when that institution collapsed in 1878, he found himself, along with too many of his countrymen—ruined!

Fortunately, however, he had previously made independent provision for his two maiden sisters; with which portion, and what was saved from the wreck, he was able to live with them in comparative comfort during the rest of his days.

He died in Brechin in 1886, aged 77; and was buried in the Cemetery there.

He took great pains, by searching Parish Registers, Charters, etc., to perfect his genealogies; in which he succeeded to a praiseworthy extent; and with considerable skill wove the result of his investigations into a consecutive story.

But in his manuscripts he occasionally interpolated notes, which he afterwards amplified in appendices, thereby causing some confusion to the reader; in order, therefore, to make the memoir plain and consecutive, without unnecessary repetition, I have mostly consolidated his notes and appendices in the text; distinguishing, however, any retained, as by the Author; against such as I have, as Editor, added myself.

Certain addenda are still given in appendices.

When Mr. Fairweather wrote his Memoir the present advanced scientific study of personal and place names had made but little progress; we, therefore, must now regard his half serious half playful speculations on the origin of the name Fairweather, as very crude and fanciful.

But, nevertheless, it is with diffidence I venture to give the following etymology of it; which at all events, whether true or not, is according to sound philology.

It may be broadly stated, with safety, that the personal name Fairweather, as we now view it, originally meant something very different from the apparent meaning of the two words of which it seems built up; both have undoubtedly undergone change in sound and spelling.

Philologists regard all old names as essentially descriptive, usually conveying definite matter of fact meaning the very opposite of fanciful; it is, therefore, necessary in order to reach the true signification of a seemingly fanciful name, to get beneath and beyond all glosses, spoken or written.

The first point certain about Fairweather is, that it is Anglic, as apart from Celtic; not merely of course, English as distinguished from Scottish; because it is common to both countries. Its chief and perhaps original centre was Danish East Anglia, especially Norfolk and Suffolk; yet, at the same time it has so long been common in East Scotland, as to have acquired a distinct Scottish association.

Now, the great mass of modern English surnames are derived from three sources, namely:

First :—Places of Residence.

Second :—Nicknames or Personal Peculiarities.

Third :—Occupations or Condition in Life.

The name of Fairweather does not apparently come under the first category; because, the only locality in the British Islands from which it could have come is Fairweather Green, near Bradford, Yorkshire; but that obscure place, (which probably ought to be in the possessive, 'Fairweather's Green') much more probably took its name from an individual, than having given it to a widely spread family.

Nor does it fit into the second category of mere nicknames; for, although the 'Fair' might be of the same order as Black, White or Brown, and, as such, form compounds like Fairbairn, Whitehead or Browning, etc.: yet, when coupled with 'weather,' what possible relevancy could it have had to a man's personal appearance or description !

We can thus only regard it as belonging to the third category—occupation or condition in life.

In this sense and derivation we must view 'Fair,' as a noun, and 'weather' as something expressed in adjective form.

There are many place names in Britain beginning in Fair,' that have no relation to the adjective 'fair'—meaning, clear, pure, light colored, etc.: but are derived from an old Norse root noun, *faar* or *fær*, meaning sheep: Thus:

Fairfield—"*faar fjall.*"= Sheep fell.

Fairgirth—"*faar garor.*"= Sheep fold.

Fairisle—"*faar ey.*"= Sheep island.

The Author mentions most suggestively, but without, of

course, the faintest suspicion of any hidden signification, certain old spellings of Fairweather in Faar and Faw, which look uncommonly like adhesion to the original Norse word for sheep.

But even if sheep were the noun, how about the adjective " weather," if adjective it be ?

The original spelling was ' vedder," which, in itself has also a Norse sound.

Now, *faar* and *vedder* combined, or substituting *w* for *ar* (Fawvedder) are just the oldest spellings of the modern name.

The Author states ' *Vedder* ' by itself is a scarce surname in some of our northern counties, long under Norse influence.

The only root for Vedder, I can trace, is that from which the word ' wether,' applied to a class of sheep, is derived. According to Chambers' Dictionary, the root is, in Anglo-Saxon, *wedher;* Icelandic, *vedher;* Danish, *wedder;* German, *widder;* of which, no doubt, the unchanging Icelandic preserves the original spelling in *v*.

The change from the old Faarvedder to the modern Fairweather is but a philological commonplace; for vowels, and the letters *v* and *w* are freely interchangeable in many languages and dialects as—in vulgar provincial English for instance—weal for veal; wictuals for victuals; vidow for widow; the dentals also *d* and *th* are in like manner often interchanged.

Now, if Fairweather be derived from the Norse roots I have mentioned, it has clearly nothing to do with atmospheric changes—fair or foul;—but is all somehow connected with sheep!

It is likely the name was originally conferred on persons whose occupation or condition in life concerned sheep; but in what sense it was so applied is doubtful; possibly, it may have been the equivalent of Shepherd, Sheepbreeder, or Sheepowner.

In curious support of this speculative derivation is the fact that, the Eastern Counties of England, where the Danes had their best foothold, and which were the chief centres of the name, are also noted for their fine flocks and breeds of sheep.

The Fairweathers, as a race, are undoubtedly Norse; or at all events Teutonic; I have never known any of them to show a Celtic strain.

The name, like Don, is at once peculiar, rare and localized; and so, readily lends itself to the investigation of the genealogist.

To me, as a Don, it has a definite consanguineous interest; for, the two families lived side by side for centuries and generations, on the lower waters of the Cruick, and frequently intermarried.

The last intermarriage was my own; whereof proof will not be wanting, while my son David Fairweather Don, lives, or his memory is preserved.

W. G. DON.

52, CANFIELD GARDENS,

LONDON, N.W.

JUNE, 1898.

THE MEMORANDUM OR HISTORY.

I.—OF THE NAME IN GENERAL.

ALL those who bear, or have borne, the rather fanciful surname of Faarvedder, Fairvodder, Fawvether, Fairvadder, Fairwither, or Fairweather, and other similar spellings, have evidently sprung from one root; but where that root was first planted; what gave rise to it; whether derived from some shrinking semi-invalid, or from one who had an inordinate craving for continual sunshine, or from an inveterate prognostication of elemental changes, can only be made a matter of conjecture, rather than of certainty; it must, therefore remain a mystery among these of the name and connection.

(NOTE by the **Editor.**—The Author, I presume, obtained these various spellings of the name from sixteenth or seventeenth century lists; written at a date when the spelling of both place and personal names was very loose and uncertain. As I have already stated, the modern Etymologist refuses to regard even the most obscure old names as either mysterious or fanciful.)

But, fortunately, the mystery is of very small moment to the bearer of the name, or anyone else; while its investigation, may, for lack of better employment, have been to the writer a profitless amusement, prompted by idle curiosity.

Whether or not, he here begs to record his sense of how imperfectly he has been able to trace back his forbears, with anything like legal accuracy, beyond the third or fourth generation; arising from the want in former times of proper parochial registers and other records of vital statistics. But there may be some consolation in the fact that at least half the people of Scotland are in similar case.

(NOTE by the **Editor.**—He might safely have said nine-tenths of the people of Scotland were in like case. How many middle-class men can name, much less trace, a great grand parent? The earliest extant Scottish parish registers date only from about the year 1600; and are very imperfect for a century later; which is not surprising when the political and religious turmoil in Scotland during the seventeenth century is considered. The registrations, moreover, could hardly be reckoned vital statistics; as Deaths were not recorded, but only Baptisms and Marriages.)

The surname Fairweather is presumably of Saxon origin, both in meaning and composition; for in the very Saxon Eastern Counties of England, especially Norfolk and Suffolk, the name is found in considerable numbers ; many of those bearing it being Tradesmen and Shopkeepers in the small towns and villages; but there must also be many others engaged in agricultural pursuits, not to be readily detected on sign-boards, and seldom found included in local Directories.

An old record shows, that, in 1604, there was one Josias Fawvedder, of Brisset, in Suffolk, who had previously lived in Henley-on-Thames. Another, of similar name, and about the same period, was a Mercer in London.

It is curious to note, that, in 1604, among the Scottish Fairweathers, there was one Jacobus of Blairno, Lethnot, Forfarshire, whose surname was also spelled Fawvedder, exactly as his English contemporaries in Suffolk and London!

(Note by the **Editor**.—This is undoubtedly more than a coincidence ; refer to remarks on the root origin.)

Moreover, the Christian name Henry, then and now common among English, was also frequent among Scottish Fairweathers; but whether that pointed to bygone affinity between the races must be left to individual opinion.

In the very Saxon Eastern Counties of England, there are many surnames with the prefix "fair" such as Fairhead, Fairmouth, etc.; there are also a number of 'Fairers;' which affords presumptive evidence that the Fairweather's are of purely Saxon origin; and that the name probably originated among the watery levels of the Eastern Counties of England, where, of course, fair-weather, would naturally be longed for, and much spoken of.

(NOTE by the **Editor.**—The Author, misled by the apparent analogy of other Saxon names, here persists in interpreting Fairweather literally, which, as I have already stated, is probably a complete mistake. Its connection with 'watery levels' and 'weeping skies,' would, for example, be pretty much on a par with an assumption that the surname Law indicated affinity to the legal profession; instead of being as we know derived from the Anglo-Saxon root, *hlaw*, a hillock!)

The migration of Fairweathers to Scotland, in the train of Norman nobles, during the twelfth and thirteenth centuries, may perhaps account for their appearance at an early date in the fertile county of Forfar, and its neighbourhood.

So far, as recorded, they have been mostly confined to that

linited area ; and do not seem, at any one period of time, during fully two centuries, to have numbered therein more than 250 to 300 males of all ages.

In September, 1873, there were of the name 26 voters on the certified roll of Dundee, besides five or six widows with families, living in the city ; in Arbroath 12, and Montrose 10 voters ; besides at least thirty to forty families scattered throughout the county.

In later years the Fairweathers have become more scattered ; some northward beyond Aberdeen ; some southward to Fife, and others westward to Perth. A limited number have also proceeded abroad; over a dozen families having, within the memory of the writer, emigrated to America, the West Indies and Australia.

There is one remarkable characteristic of the Fairweathers ; that, during the 350 years in which they can be traced, not one of the name has even approached distinction in the realms of learned life or of the fine arts. But while the fact can be freely admitted, there is some compensation, in that very few have been vicious, and hardly one has sunk into criminal depravity ; or, while neither famed for wealth nor high position have they seldom descended to poverty.

(NOTE by the **Editor**.—Sweeping generalizations of this kind were better avoided; because, if broadly are seldom literally true. The Fairweathers having attained and maintained for many generations a good average middle-class moral and material respectability, must therefore have possessed fair average intellectual capacity. How many superlatively distinguished citizens have the great family of Smith, for instance—numbering 1 in 74 of the total Scottish population—produced? Yet, if undistinguished, a vast number of our best citizens bear and have borne that common name. The persistency of a family, or race, is, in the end, of far more importance than its brilliancy. The tendency of all families, who rise above the herd, is to deteriorate and become extinct: but those who have successfully resisted that tendency—like the Fairweathers—for many generations, do show at least superior innate nervous organization. Families which produce geniuses seldom long survive in the community.)

While Agriculture seems to have been the favorite, chosen, occupation of the race, yet, not a few have risen to municipal distinction in urban communities. In Dundee, some were respectable Burgesses and Magistrates, two and even three centuries ago; and the same remark applies to the Burghs of Brechin and Forfar.

(NOTE by the **Editor.**—In Black's History of Brechin, the following appear among the Town Councillors:—And : Fairweather, Councillor, 1682.—Alexander Fairweather, Councillor and Hospital Master, 1691-98 ; Bailie 1699 to 1703 ; Dean of Guild, 1705.—An Alexander Fairweather, signs as a Witness in the Brechin Register, to the baptism of Alexander, son of James Don, in 1657.)

Although few Fairweathers figure in the learned professions, yet one of the oldest recorded was a Lawyer ; Walter Fairweather, Notary and Presbyter of the Diocese of Dunkeld, about 1547 ; whose name occurs in connection with lands held by that See in Menmuir. He witnessed, and probably drafted (in Latin) at least three Charters, connected with the Estate of Findowrie, which then marched with, or was more likely partly included in, Menmuir. In one of the Deeds he is called ' Schir Valtro Fairvedder,' a title of civil knighthood not uncommon among high placed Churchmen before the Reformation.

In the Clerical Profession the following names appear.— The Revd. Thomas Fairweather, of Forfarshire, graduated at King's College, Aberdeen, along with Alexander Arbuthnott, Junior, of Findowrie, 1675. The Revd. Alexander Fairweather,

Maybole, 1696, was a Jacobite, and, in consequence, forced to resign his living; he was afterwards for a short time at Inverkeithing, but returned to and died at Maybole in 1740.

The Revd. Robert Fairweather was helper at Cortachy 1693, was inducted at Carnbee, Fife, in 1693, and translated to Crail. 1701. He was twice married; first to Ann, daughter of Pat Lindsay, third in the line of Hormiston and Balcarres, Fife, (a property still in the family), and had a son named Patrick; secondly to Rachael Bethune. He died in 1718.

The Revd. Robert Fairweather, Parish Minister of Nigg, Kincardinshire, was ordained in 1889.

The Revd. Alexander Fairweather, Free Church, Brotriphine, Moray, was ordained in 1843.

The Revd. William Fairweather, of the Presbyterian Church, Newcastle-on-Tyne, died some years ago.

A Thomas Fairweather, teacher at the same place, was, judging from a recent obituary notice, a man held in high esteem in the community.

(Note by the **Editor.**—In addition to the above there are now, also, (1898.) the Revd. William Fairweather, Free Church, Maryton, Montrose; the Revd. William Fairweather, Free

Church, Dunnikier; and the Revd. David Fairweather, a very rising Free Church Minister, native of the Kirriemuir or Dundee district.

In the Medical Profession, the only representative is Dr. James Fairweather, of the Menmuir stock, who promises a good career in the Indian service.

(NOTE by the Editor.—There is another medical representative since the Author wrote, David Fairweather, M.A., M.D., of the Langhaugh family, an eminent practitioner at Wood Green, London. There are also others of the name (untraced) now in the Medical Directory.)

The Military Profession has only had one Commissioned representative in the regular army; namely, Major Thomas Fairweather, 21st Regiment, Royal Scots Fusiliers, who died in Edinburgh in 1845. After retirement he settled in Australia; but being unfortunate returned to Scotland. He left daughters but no son; and his family connections are untraced.

(NOTE by the Editor—The Author here overlooked the fact, that Dr. James Fairweather, was a Commissioned Officer in the Indian Forces. There are now several of the name holding Commissions in the Volunteer Force.)

II.—OF THE ANGUS FAIRWEATHERS.

HE localities in Forfarshire, where the race has been longest and most thickly settled, are as follows:—

(1)   **Menmuir,**—before 1547.

(2)   **Dundee,**—before 1583.

(3)   **Brechin,**

(4)   **Glamis,**

(5)   **Forfar,**   First half of the Seventeenth Century.

(6)   **Kirriemuir.**

Outside Forfarshire, a Messenger of Court, named Fairweather, is mentioned at Falkland, Fife, in 1591; and one of the name recorded at Forgue, in Aberdeenshire, in 1658.

The following early notices are extracted from Deeds and Charters recorded in the Chartulary of the Diocese of Brechin; and from the old Kirk Session Book of Menmuir:—

(1) In an ' Instrument of Donation of Assignation of the ' lands of Finlarg, in the Parish of Tealing, to the Church ' of Brechin,' one **Robert Wedyr** is mentioned, in 1453. (Vol. II., page 95.)

Note by the Author.—As no other instance of the surname Wedyr is to be found at any time, near or remote, in the district; and, as Fairvedders were living near Dundee, about a century later, may not this Robert have been an early progenitor; with his name for some reason abbreviated? In some of our Northern Counties there is still a scarce surname ‘Vedder.’

(Note by the Editor.—As before explained, the letters *r* and *w* are and long have been, interchangeable; it is therefore, not at all improbable Wedyr’s real name was Vedder; and it is further possible the ‘fair’ had been docked from it; for very curious liberties were often taken with names in old documents, especially if written in Latin.)

(2) ‘15th Januarie 1547, Instrument Sasine (conveyance or ‘infeftment of land) in the favor of William Dempster of ‘Carraldstone (Careston), witnessed by William Lyon of ‘Easter Ogil; William Lyell of Murthell; George Falconer; ‘David Ferstone; and Robert Hutone, cum diversis aliis. ‘**Valtro Fairvedder**, presbyterno Dunkaldense, diocesi notario.’

(3) ‘3rd December, 1551, Reception Sasine, favorem Roberti ‘Cullace de Balnamunes, et Suæ spousæ, terrarum de Fyndowrie.

' **Valtro Fairvedder,** et Herbert Gladstanys, et notarii diversi
' aliis.'

' (Signed) David Fentone, with my hand, fear of Ogil.'

(Note by the **Editor.**—The latter Reception was the complete
conveyance of the lands of Findowrie to the laird of Balnamoon through his wife; and is dated about the time when
church lands were largely assigned to neighbouring proprietors.
' Fear' that is, Fee-ar or Fiar, feudal proprietor of Ogil.   It
is interesting to note that the name ' Herbert' occurs in Mr.
W. E. Gladstone's family to this day !)

(4) " 22nd May, 1583.—Warrandice (authority, security) of
' the lands of Findowry by David Fentone, to Robert Cullace
' and his spouse ; said obligation is subscribed, at Balnamone,
' the 16th day of February, 1562, before witnesses ; viz. :
' Robert Cullace younger ; Henrie Chalmers, John Scott, and
' **Schir Walter Fairvedder,** notary public, and registered in the
' Sheriff Court Books at Forfar the 22nd day of May, 1563.'

Note by the Author.—Before the Reformation it was not
uncommon for Churchmen of a certain rank to be designated
somewhat the same as Military Knights.   John Knox himself
is an instance ; when he was a Popish Priest he also acted

as a Notary in Haddington, and witnessed as 'Schir' John Knox.

(NOTE by the Editor.—The last extract was evidently the final legal warrant, or ratification, of the lands of Findowrie to Cullace of Balnamoon; connected with the transfer of 1551. Sir Walter Fairvedder must have lived to be an old man, for he figures in these 'instruments' during forty years. The Charters are in dog legal Latin.)

Passing to Dundee, in the 'Howff' burying ground there, on the western border, is a very old flat monumental stone, with an inscription rapidly becoming obliterated. It is to the Memory of **Thomas** and **Robert Fairvedder**—probably father and son; the latter was a Litster, or Dyer. The former is recorded to have died in 1583, aged 44, and the latter in 1609; a curious monogram of Roberts' is copied from the gravestone, in 'Jervise's Memorials of Angus and Mearns.'

In the same 'Howff' there was, or still is, another gravestone, with the following record:—" Here resteth in the Lord, " **William** and **George Fairweathers**, Skippers; of pious, virtuous " and upright life, who lived with the love of all persons, and " at their death were much lamented, (the father deceased 13th

' May, 1683, of his age 61; the son dying 25th May, 1683,
" of age 32), and Katherine Constable, spouse of **William Fair-**
" **weather,** the younger, a religious, virtuous young woman, is
" also here interred, who deceased 11th May, 1684. Her
" age 20."

A third gravestone lies in the middle of the ' Howff,' and is
partly defaced. It has a Latin inscription to **James Fairweather,**
a citizen of wealth and consequence in Dundee ; for he held
mortgages over the estates of Lord Northesk, and had been
Provost of the Burgh.

The inscription runs thus :

" No 555. Here are laid the ashes of **James Fairweather,** a
" singularly honest and moderately successful Merchant in this
" Town. He was Provost, and bore other honours connected
" with that dignity. There were none of the Christian virtues
" which he did not greatly love, and constantly cultivate. When
" he died he had lived 68 years. He died on the 5th day of
" December, in the year 1738."

" With the ashes of his father, here rests what was mortal
of **John Fairweather,** Merchant and Bailie of Dundee, who
" was held in great respect for his religion and truth, as one

" who avoided every false way. He was born 14th May, 1706,
" and died 31st July, 1760. Bailie, 1738 and 1740."

The right to the burial place of Provost Fairweather, passed
in the female line to another family resident in Montreal. The
older burying ground of Thomas and Robert is widely sepa-
rated from that of the Provost. James was Bailie about 1716,
and twice Provost, 1723-29, and 1732-33; it is not known
whether he was any relation of a **Thomas Fairweather** who
was also Bailie in Dundee, 1706.

(NOTE by the **Editor.**—These records show there were sub-
stantial citizens of the name in Dundee, for two hundred
years, between 1550 and 1750.)

Reverting to the Parish of Menmuir and neighbourhood,
there is no mention of Fairweathers, (although they undoubtedly existed) between 1563 and 1609. But, in the latter year,
there is an entry in a Latin Charter of an annual donation
of " 6 sh. 8 pence," for some object; witnessed by ' Joanes
' Ramsay, Commissario Brechinensis; Jacobo Stratown in
' Drumcairne; **Jacobo Fawvedles** in Blairno; Jacobo Johnstone
' in Glastone; et William Setone, servitor ipsias; Pauli Fraser,
' 17th April, 1609.'

There is good reason to believe that this Latinized 'Faw-veddles' was indeed Fawvedder, for a family of Fairweathers were long in occupation of that farm, in Lethnot; the last of whom, **Alexander Fairweather,** died there in June, 1741. He, on 27th September, 1730, married Jean Mitchell, of Menmuir; by whom he had male children; for there is evidence of their having received a classical (college ?) education; but their after history is unknown. Jean, his widow afterwards married William Speid; who, through her, obtained the tenancy of Blairno; and whose descendents, by a subsequent marriage, held it for over a century.

(NOTE by the **Editor.**—The Latinizing of common Saxon and Celtic names in old documents is often carried to such a ridiculous extent, that it is next to impossible to recognise them. No doubt Fawvedles, for Fawvedder, is an example of such pedantry.)

A curious document was lately discovered among the Panmure Papers in connection with 'Jacobo Fawvedles' of Blairno, entitled: 'Ane Assignation or Disposition, perfected be the 'Gudeman Wishart, of Drimmies, and his son, with consent 'of the Earl of Marr,' (the then proprietor of the Lordships of Brechin and Navar; namely, John, seventh Earl, the early friend and companion of James the Sixth, who in his usual playful manner, nick-named him, "Jockie o' Sclates,") 'to 'Hendrie Farewaddire, and his two sons, James and John, anent 'the Wadset of the lands of Blairno; at Brechin, 8th August, '1611.' (A Wadset is a legal document by which a debtor gives over his heritable subjects into the hands of his creditors.)

This document fixes the settlement of the Fairweathers of Blairno, on or before 1609, and perfected 1611; in that farm the family remained as tenants until June, 1741, a period of 132 years.

But it gives also, through the oldest Session Book of Menmuir (1622), a clue to other points of interest; for the very first name mentioned in that book is 'Hendrie Fairvedder,' no doubt one and the same with 'Hendrie Farewaddire' of the deed.

It may thus be safely asumed that, in 1611, this Hendrie was at least 50 years of age; for his sons James and John had then fully reached man's estate. From him and this date we begin the· descent of the Menmuir Fairweathers.

We have no specific record of his two sons; but a com-

parison of dates and other recorded names warrant the follow-
conclusions :—

James as the elder, and in virtue of the Wadset; no doubt
succeeded in the tenancy of Blairno, but we have no record
of his wife or children. John, the younger's, history is likewise obscure; but the sequence in dates goes to show that he
was the father of a second John, and of a second Hendrie ;
for in 1644, twenty years after the commencement of the
Session Book, (thirty-three years after the ' Wadset,') John
Fairvedder, of Blackhall, and Hendrie Fairwedder, of Braco, are
ennumerated with seventeen other names on the roll of Elders.
The elderly Hendrie of 1612, could hardly have been the Kirk
Elder of 1644 ; and it is equally improbable the two Johns
were one and the same individual.

The Hendrie of Braco, moreover, had a son named 'Alexander,' baptised 8th April, 1649, and figured as Kirk Treasurer
between 1668 and 1670,

The John of Blackhall, had a daughter named 'Janet,'
baptised 30th July, 1648, and in 1661, was deputed to act as
an Elder at a provincial Synod held at Forfar ; he was further
named as Kirk Treasurer in 1676.

These various dates, therefore, go to prove the existence of two Johns and two Hendries beyond any doubt.

Furthermore, the lineal descent here shown is corroborated and almost demonstrated from contemporary evidence. John Fairwedder, of Blackhall, was the father of the family party mentioned on the memorial stone, now built into the south wall of Menmuir Church, and which is dedicated to the memory of ' their Ancestors Residenters In this Paroch.'

This reference to ancestors clearly indicates that the Fair-weathers had long been settled in Menmuir and the adjoining districts.

Note by the Editor.—The Author here, in so far as his information warranted, balances dates very adroitly. Adopting his estimates that, in 1609, Hendrie, of Blairno, must have been 50 or 60 years of age, it is not difficult to work out an approximate date table of these early ancestors, as follows :

(1)	**Hendrie** 1st, (Blairno)	...	1550 to 1620.
(2)	**James** ,,	...	1580 to 1650.
(3)	**John** 1st, (?)	...	1582 to 1652.
(4)	**John** 2nd, (Blackhall)	...	1613 to 1676
(5)	**Hendrie** 2nd (Braco)	...	1612 to 1680.

I fix the death of John, of Blackhall, about 1676; because he then ceased to be mentioned in the Session Book; and, as other entries show, about that time was succeeded in the tenancy of Blackhall by James Don, who had married his daughter Isabel, in whom the life rent of the farm was vested.)

From various records it is very probable the Fairweathers of Blairno, Lethnot, were offshoots of the Menmuir stock, which at the beginning of the seventeenth century were fairly numerous in the parish; for, contemporary with John of Blackhall and Hendrie of Blaco, there were others of the name, untraced and unidentified, as shown in the following entries in the Session Book:

John Fairvedder, of Brathinch, had a daughter baptised Magdalene, 2nd September, 1648. **John Fairvedder**, at Crossbank, Balnamoon, 1644; **David Fairvedder**, 1648; both received donations. The Bairns of **James Fairvedder**, 1668, and of **Thomas Fairvedder**, June 1672, being in necessitous circumstances, received allowances of meal.

In September, 1678, it is recorded that one Robert Murray had to do penance before the Kirk Session for ' Slandering ' an **Alexander Fairvedder,** who was no doubt a *persona grata* in the Kirk; and who, ten years later, 1688, apparently reappears, under the spelling **Alexander Ffairweather,** as the borrower of ' 20 lib ' from Kirk Session funds, which accommodation he did not repay in a hurry, as it was outstanding in 1694.

In 1679, and again in 1681, it is recorded that an Elder, named **Andrew Fairweather,** who seems to have been a Miller, repaid in meal, money which he had borrowed from the Kirk Session.

(NOTE by the **Editor.**—These entries show that, in the Seventeenth Century there were many Fairweathers in Menmuir in widely different pecuniary circumstances. The lending of Kirk Session Funds to Elders seems to us a curious and doubtful proceeding; but in those days there were no banks from which to borrow in necessity.)

Although there is no record, the above Andrew was probably miller at the Mill of Blackhall, and a son of John the tenant; also, that the ' Slandered ' Alexander was his brother; further, it is probable that one or other of these men were father to Alexander in Little Cruick, and George in in Milltoun of Balhall, brothers, who figure on the Menmuir monument.

(NOTE by the **Editor.**—This is the only occasion in which the Author favours the surmise that the Alexander and George of the monument were grandsons of John of Blackhall, and not sons. That they were grandsons I have no doubt; because, on no other supposition can a number of collateral dates and facts be made to fit in.

It is very likely John's sons, Andrew and Alexander, were Millers, sub-tenants of their father; for, on Cruick Water, even down to my own time, the millers were usually sons of the tenants of the various farms. Now, James Don, who succeeded John Fairweather in the tenancy of Blackhall, after 1676, had a son, also named James, who, for a number of years during his father's lifetime, was always designated in the Menmuir Register, as 'younger' of, or at, Blackhall; and who probably succeeded the Fairweathers as Miller. I hold it was this 'younger' James who is mentioned on the Menmuir monument; because he is described 'Att the Mill of Blackhall;' had it been his father, the older James, he would of course have been spoken of as 'in' Blackhall, like other actual tenants.

Holding that Alexander and George of the monument were

grandsons of John, by Andrew the Miller, or Alexander the 'Slandered,' then, there is strong probability that James Don and Alexander Smith, also mentioned on the Monument, were likewise his grandsons; the four men, therefore, would primarily be first cousins; and secondly, as the Author supposes, may also have been brothers-in-law through intermarriage with Fair-weathers. I have gone into these questions in the Don Memoirs, and think the Author, through defective information, did not discriminate sufficiently between the Dons and Smiths, senior and junior. This will come out as the history is unfolded.)

The Menmuir Memorial Stone, which is an important factor in this history, bears the following inscription :

" 1717. This monument was erected at the charge and " expense of Alexander Fairweather, In Little Cruick, George " Fairweather, In Milltown of Balhall, James Don, att the Mill " of Blackhall, and Alexander Smith, in Teagertown, in " Memory of their Ancestors, Residenters In this Paroch, and " for themselves, wives, children and their posterity."

" Fearst thou faint Heart, that narrow plank to pass,

" Which Christ himself hath had, which all men must;

" That like a child held by the sleeve, thou go'st;

" Beyond it thou shall see these pleasant plains,

" Whose boundless Beauty all discourse transcendeth ;

" Where Kings and Subjects souls hath equal Reigns

" On blessed Thrones, where glory never Endeth."

On a narrow panel below is " Memento Mori," with mortuary and husbandry emblems. Also, " Thomas Don, " Wright in Duninald, died 1809," which of course had been added a century after the original inscriptions.

The fact that this stone was originally built into the Church wall, and replaced there in 1842, indicates that the Fairweathers it commemorates had long been residents of good position in Menmuir.

(NOTE by the **Editor.**—I doubt if the stone was originally inserted in the wall; this is the account of it I had from David Fairweather, of Langhaugh. Sometime before 1840, Robert Don, of Brechin, contracted for the repair of the Church of Menmuir ; and during operations, finding the stone derelict in the churchyard, with true filial instinct, built it into the wall on his own initiative. Years afterwards its prominent position offended the taste of a new minister, who wished to remove it ; but the factor to the chief heritor intervened and told him politely but firmly to leave it alone.)

Note by the Author.—There is the strongest probability that the brothers Fairweather mentioned on the monument, with their sisters, married to James Don and Alexander Smith, were sons and daughters of John Fairvedder, in Blackhall, who himself was son of John second son of Hendrie of Blairno, as appears from the following sequence of dates:—If John of Blackhall was born, say in 1610, he would only have been 66 when last mentioned in the Session Book, 1676; he had a child baptised in 1648; and, if the oldest Fairweather, mentioned on the monument had been born, say in 1650, then he would only have been about 70 when his son succeeded him in Little Cruick in 1719; while John's youngest daughter, 'Keatren,' wife of Alexander Smith, born 1662, died 1702, would, had she lived, been only 57 in 1719.

(Note by the Editor.—I have already expressed dissent from these conclusions of the Author; on account of the impossibility of fitting them into the contemporary Don record, which is as follows:

James Don, second son of Thomas of Dalbog, was about 20 years of age in 1672, when, as recorded on the Edzell tombstone, his father died.

He appears to have married Isobel, daughter of John Fairvedder of Blackhall about 1676, and, through her succeeded to the tenancy of the farm, about that date.

The Menmuir Register, beginning in 1704, records that, of the children of this marriage, Margaret married John Gald, in 1705; while Charles and James had children baptised in 1707; and Arthur children later on. James Don had thus grown up sons, with families, ten years before the Menmuir Monument was erected. Only James, of his sons, concerns us here; his wife's name is unrecorded, but she probably was a cousin Fairweather; he had a large family between 1707 and 1728; and up to his father's death in 1724, is always described in the Register as 'younger,' at of, or in Blackhall; which indicates he was at home with his father, probably as a sub-tenant and Miller; which would account for his being described on the Monument as, 'Att 'the Mill of Blackhall.' In 1717 he was probably about 35 years of age, and was thus old enough, and in a position to share the expense of the Monument, and be recorded thereon. That this 'younger' James was the Don of the Monument I have no doubt; because, had it been his father, as the Author supposes, he could not in speaking of a deceased wife describe her as an 'ancestor.'

Isobel Fairweather, James the 'younger's' mother, died about 1690; for, at that date, as my father records, the life rent of Blackhall lapsed; but it was then renewed on a first nineteen year's lease, and again in 1709 on a second, which finally terminated in 1728, when the Don's left Blackhall.

James Don, senior, married about 1698, his second wife, Isobel Fyfe; who was mother to Alexander, born 1700, afterwards tenant in Ballownie, 1742.

Now, as it may reasonably be held, the men mentioned on the Monument were age contemporaries, it could hardly be that Alexander and George Fairweather, and Alexander Smith were uncles to James Don; rather, all four were first cousins, perhaps brothers-in-law, and men in middle life. This theory finds support in the fact that Keatren Fairweather, the mother of Alexander Smith, Junior, (see Appendix) died in 1702, fifteen years before the Monument was erected.)

Through the Fairweathers mentioned on the Monument are descended the existing two important local branches of the name; from Alexander in Little Cruick have come the Menmuir Fairweathers; from George of Milltown of Balhall are the Fairweathers which may be designated of Brechin.

Alexander Fairweather, in Little Cruick (about 1676), was succeeded in that farm at his death in 1719, by a son named George, (wife not named) who had the following children :—

(1)   **Jean,**   baptised   ...   November, 1719.

(2)   **Margaret,**   ,,   ...   October, 1721.

(3)   **Isobel,**   ,,   ...   February, 1723.

(4)   **Anne,**   ,,   ...   June, 1725.

(5)   **George,**   ,,   ...   February, 1728.

(6)   **Agnes,**   ,,   ...   April, 1730.

(7)   **Alexander,**   ,,   ...   June, 1732.

(7) **Alexander** succeeded his father in Little Cruick, and Langhaugh, about 1760, and married Catherine Dargie, by whom he had the following children :—

(1)   **John,** 1759 to 1825, (succeeded in the combined farms.)

(2)   **David,**   (unmarried, Merchant in Brechin.)

(3)   **Alexander,**   (untraced, went to London.)

(4)   **Helen,**   (married James Mitchell.)

(5)   **Jessie.**

(6)   **James.**

(7)   **Magdelene.**

(1) **John**, of Langhaugh and Little Cruick, married Ann Rickard, daughter of Alexander Rickard, in Lochtie; and died in 1825, aged 66; his wife died, August, 1853, aged 66 years. They had a numerous family, but all died in infancy, except two:

(1) **Elizabeth,** 1810 to 1894, unmarried.

(2) **David,** 1819 to 1890.

(2) **David**, Farmer, Langhaugh, married, 1851, Isabella, youngest daughter of David Webster, Mill of Balrownie, and Jean Don, his wife, daughter of Alexander Don, Ballownie, and had the following children:

(1) **Jean Ann,** born 9th April, 1852.

(2) **Isabella,** ,, 4th October, 1853.

(3) **David,** ,, 16th April, 1855.

(4) **John,** ,, 26th May, 1857.

(5) **Elizabeth Mary,** ,, 3rd April, 1863.

(1) **Jean**, married 26th June, 1889, William Gerard Don, (the writer), M.D., Deputy Surgeon-General, Army, youngest son of Alexander Don, Ballownie, her cousin once removed, and had two sons; one still-born, January, 1891; and David Fairweather Don, born 23rd August, 1893.

(2) **Isabella**, married, 1881, William Jackson Kennedy, M.D., of Kirkcaldy, (who died, 1888, and is buried in Brechin Ceme-

tery), and had a daughter, Isabella Fairweather Kennedy, born 24th October, 1887.

(3) **David**, M.A., M.D., of Edinburgh University, of Wood Green, London, married, 5th February, 1898, Jeanie Miller, widow of W. Urquhart Weldon.

(4) **John**, Farmer, Chapelton, unmarried, (1898.)

(5) **Elizabeth**, married, 10th January, 1889, John Adamson, of Adamson and McTaggart, Merchants, Negapatam, Madras, (who died in India, 19th May, 1890), and had a son, John, born at Pulnai Hills, Madras, 15th August, 1890.

NOTE by the Author.—David, of Langhaugh, is (1874) the undoubted head and representative of the Menmuir race, and also the last of the family resident in the district.

(NOTE by the **Editor**.—David died suddenly of apoplexy, 12th May, 1890, aged 72. He was a middle-sized, stout, reddish fair, blue-eyed, hale and hearty man; of polished manners, quick intelligence, and of the highest honour and integrity; especially will his unvarying geniality and remarkable fund of humour be cherished by those who knew him intimately. For many years, and up to the time of his death, he was an Elder of the Menmuir Free Church.)

George Fairweather (of the Monument) Milltown of Balhall, died probably between 1720 and 1725; and left at least two sons,

(1) Alexander.

(2) George.

(1) Alexander, of Waukmill, near Milltown of Ballhall, had the following children :—

(1) George, baptised, May, 1719.   (Accidently killed while young.)

(2)   Elizabeth,   ,,   January, 1721.

(3)   Helen,   ,,   February, 1723.

(4)   Alexander,   ,,   July, 1727.

(5)   Janet,   ,,   1729.

(6)   Anne,   ,,   March, 1731.

(7)   John,   ,,   February, 1733.

Their history is unrecorded, except :

(4) Alexander, settled in Brechin, and married, first, his cousin (?) Janet Don, daughter of Alexander Don, Black-hall, Ireland and Ballownie, and by her had :

(1) Janet, who became second wife to Andrew Leighton Farmer, Syde Stracathro.

(2)   Katherine, married John Marr, Forfar.

(3)   **Elizabeth,** married David Kerr, Brechin.

(4)   **Margaret,** died unmarried.

(5)   **William,** Merchant, Dundee.

By his second wife, Margaret Anderson, Alexander had three daughters.

(5) **William,** of Dundee, married Agnes Petrie, and had four daughters, and the following three sons :—

(1)   **William,** District Registrar, Dundee.

(2)   **Alexander,** Free Church Minister, Botriphnie.

(3)   **James,** Merchant, Dundee.

(1)   **William,** District Registrar, died 21st September, 1860, and by his wife Euphemia Watt, had :

(1)   **William.**

(2)   **Alexander**

(3)   **Charles.**

(4)   **James.**

(5)   **John.**

(6)   **Agnes.**

(7)   **Euphemia.**

(8)   **Jane.**

Of the members of this large family recorded :

(1) **William** married Mary Gilchrist, and had four sons and two daughters.

(2) **Alexander**, (The Reverend), died June 24th, 1869; married Elizabeth Clark, who died, January, 1861, and had issue:

(1) **Thomas.**

(2) **Agnes.**

(1) **Thomas**, Merchant, Mintlaw, Aberdeen, married Mary Morrison, and had children.

(4) **James**, died 1st March, 1869, married Catherine Dewar, and had:

(1) **William.**

(2) **James.**

(2) **Elizabeth.**

(4) **Margaret Jane.**

George, second son of George of the Monument, succeeded in Milltown of Balhall, and married, as his first wife, Jean Brand, daughter of William Brand, Mains of Findowrie, and by her had children baptised as follows:

(1) **George**, November, 1725.

(2) **Jean**, July, 1725.

(3) **Alexander**, August, 1729.

(4)   **William,** November, 1781.

(Parish Register then blank.)

(5)   **Margaret.**

(6)   **Isobel.**

(7)   **Anne.**

(1)   **George,** in Kirkton of Menmuir, died young, unmarried.

(2)   **Jean,** married John Skair, Bogton of Balhall.

(3)   **Alexander,** in Balzeordie, died unmarried 1794.

(4)   **William,** in Mill of Brathinch, died about 1795. He had three daughters, one of whom married David Valentine, Brechin, and had a large family.

(5)   **Margaret,** first wife of David Leighton, Burnhead.

(6)   **Isobel,** married Alexander Don, and was the mother of George Don, the eminent Forfar Botanist; besides another son and five daughters.

(NOTE by the **Editor.**—This Alexander, son of James Don (younger) in Blackhall, was born in 1717, and, living to be almost a centenarian, died 1813. He married Isobel Fairweather in 1760, and his second child was the celebrated George, born 1764, died 1814. The botanist was not born in Forfar, as generally stated, but at Ireland, in Menmuir, which his father farmed. Alexander was much older than his wife, who, according to my genealogy, was his cousin once removed; and grand-daughter of George Fairweather, of the Monument.)

(7) **Anne,** married Thomas Leighton, Brechin, second son of David Leighton, in Balrownie, and had issue:

(1) **Annie,** died unmarried.

(2) **Margaret,** married George Fairweather.

(3) **David,** (Sir David Leighton, K.C.B.)

(4) **Magdelene,** died unmarried.

(2) **Margaret,** in 1795, married George Fairweather, (of the Kirriemuir Fairweathers), late tenant in Brathinch, and had four sons and four daughters.

(1) **David.**

(2) **James.**

'3) **George.**

(4) **Alexander,** (writer of this History.)

(5) **Anne.**

(6) **Jean.**

(7) **Margaret.**

(8) **Elizabeth.**

All of this large family died unmarried.

(3) David (Leighton) entered the service of the Honourable

East India Company, and rose to be a distinguished General Officer, Sir David Leighton, K.C.B. He married in 1818, Isabella Constantia Williams, and had two sons, David Russell, Merchant, Manchester; Edmund Thomas, M.D., London; and three daughters; Honoria Flora, Amelia Mary, and Isabella.

George, of Milltown of Balhall, married, as his second wife, Margaret Leighton, daughter of John Leighton, Farmer, Coull, and had issue:

(1) **David.**

(2) **James.**

(3) **Janet.**

(4) **Elizabeth.**

(5) **George,** (shown in the resumed Menmuir Register, as baptised 1st February, 1759.)

(1) **David,** tenant in Balzeordie, married, 1787, Anne Watt, and by her had issue:

(1) **James,** born April, 1788, died July, 1870.

(2) **John,** born 1790, died unmarried, 1817.

(3) **Jean,** born 1792, died unmarried, 1817.

(4) **George,** born 1797, died abroad.

(1) **James,** succeeded in Balzeordie, and afterwards, for forty-five years, was superintendent of the brewing department, North

Port Distillery, Brechin. He married Anne, daughter of John Black, Farmer, Vane, and had issue :

(1)   **David**, died unmarried, at Rothesay, 1893.

(2)   **Annie**, died unmarried at Rothesay, 1893.

(3)   **Jane.**

(4)   **James**, Doctor of Medicine.

(5)   **Isabella**.

(6)   **Mary.**

(4) **James** studied medicine, as a pupil of Alexander Guthrie, Surgeon, Brechin, and at Edinburgh University, where he graduated in 1853. He entered the service of the Honourable East India Company, in 1855; and after a successful career retired in 1886; with the rank of Deputy Surgeon General. He subsequently became private medical adviser to the Rajah of Kapurthala, where he now (1898) resides, in India. He married, in 1870, Annette Thorpe, and had the following children :

(1)   **Winifred Anne Sarah**, married Andrew McCormick, Lieutenant, Royal Engineers, 1896.

(2)   **Aleen Margaret Jane.**

(3)   **James Courtney Thorpe**, in the Indian Police.

(4)   Neville Edward, (tea-planter in India.)

(5)   Ethel Rosalie.

(6)   Arthur Dupré.

(7)   Annette Violet.

(8)   Harold.

(9)   Ian.

(2) James (of the second Balhall family) tenant in Shand-ford, Fearn, married Clarabella Alexander, and had issue:

(1)   Alexander, died young, unmarried.

(2)   Jean.

(3)   Elizabeth.

(4)   Mary.

(5)   Anne.

(6)   Agnes.

(7)   James, married with a family.

(8)   John,   do.   do.

(9)   David,   do.   do.   .

(3) Janet, married John Baxter, Tigerton, Menmuir, and had issue three sons and a daughter.

(4) Elizabeth, married James Webster, Farmer, Smiddyhill, Stracathro. No issue.

(5) George, Farmer. Pitdreichie, Kincardinshire, born in

1759, died in 1845.　Married Isabel Wishart, and had issue :

(1)　　George.

(2)　　David.

(3)　　Isabella.

(4)　　Elizabeth.

(1)　George, Farmer, Drumsleed, married, in 1841, Elizabeth Crabb, (died 1874), and had issue :

(1)　　George.

(2)　　David, died young, leaving widow and two children, all dead.

(3)　　Elsie, died 1859.

APPENDIX I.

Memorandum on the Fairweathers of Kirriemuir.

CONSIDERABLE branch, numerically, of Fairweathers, apparently settled in Kirriemuir, and adjoining parts, long ago. But the records in the Parish Kirk Session Book are very meagre. The following (baptisms only) are registered:—

(1) Child of Andrew Fairweather.

    1. Jean, 1720.

(2) Children of Francis Fairweather, Millhead of Kirriemuir.

    1. Margaret, 1720.

    2. Elizabeth.

(3) Children of John Fairweather, in Bents.

    1. Helen, 1721.

    2. Agnes, 1724.

    3. David, 1727.

(4) Children of James Fairweather, in Garlow.

1. James,

2. Christan,

              1731 to 1740

3. John,

4. David,

(5) Children of Alexander Fairweather, in Cottertoun of Shielhill.

1. Janet,

2. Alexander,

3. Robert,

              1736 to 1751.

4. James,

5. Agnes,

6. Charles,

(6) Child of Ludovick Fairweather, Muirside of Glaswell.

1. Thomas, 1739.

(7) Child of Alexander Fairweather, Wester Bog.

(1) Margaret, 1752.

John Fairweather, in Bents, (now merged in Migvie and Longbank), died soon after the birth of his son David. His widow married Alexander Millar, Farmer, Migvie, and their descendents continued prominent agriculturists, in Migvie, Ballinshoe, Inverquharity, etc., to about the beginning of the present century. His son, David, in Knowhead, (now merged in Easter Ogil, Tannadice), married 1755, Isobel Hood, and died in 1772, leaving a young family of five sons (and two daughters), namely:

1. David.

2. James.

3. George.

4. Alexander.

5. Charles.

Alexander died in London unmarried; but the other brothers left numerous families.

George was tenant in Brathinch, Menmuir, and, as before stated in the Memoirs, married Margaret Leighton, daughter of Thomas Leighton and Anne Fairweather, Brechin; thereby effecting a link between the Kirriemuir and Menmuir branches of the name. Of his numerous family was Alexander, Author of these Memoirs.

APPENDIX II.

Intermarriage between the 'Dons,' 'Fairweathers,' and 'Leightons' of the Menmuir District.

(NOTE by the Editor.—As the Author's account of this inter-connection is not only imperfect but incorrect, I will not reproduce it, but give one of my own.)

THE first known intermarriage is that of James Don, son of Thomas Don, Dalbog, Edzell, with Isabel, daughter of John Fairvedder, in Blackhall, Menmuir, of date probably about 1676. Their recorded children, given in the Don Memoirs, as mentioned in the Menmuir Register, were Margaret, Charles, James, and Arthur. This son James, who, apparently was Miller 'att the Mill of Blackhall,' was always registered in the baptisms of his numerous children, as 'younger,' of Blackhall, up to his father's death in 1724. I have already given my reasons for regarding him as the James Don of the Menmuir Monument, and that he, like the two Fairweathers and the Smith mentioned thereon, was a grandson of old John Fairvedder, while all the four were cousins. Whether he was also a brother-in-law of the Fairweathers is not known, but probable; and, if so, his would constitute intermarriage number two. James, 'younger,' had a son Alexander, born in 1717, who, in 1760, married his cousin (removed) Isobel, daughter of George Fairweather, in Milltoun of Balhall, who figures on the Monument; this would constitute intermarriage number three, from which sprang the ' Botanist' Dons.

James Don, 'younger,' had a half-brother Alexander, (mother's name Isobel Fyfe), ultimately in Ballownie, and a leading progenitor of the Dons. He was three times married, and his second wife (1731) Janet Leighton, was, according to Alexander Fairweather, widow of John Fairweather, Inishewan, Tannadice; and through her were the 'Bonnyhard Dons'; this constituted the first Leighton intermarriage. She had a daughter, Janet Don, who, according to the Brechin Register, married in 1757, Alexander Smith, Farmer, Pitpoukes; but, according to Alexander Fairweather, was the first wife of Alexander Fairweather, Brechin, son of one of the same name in Waukmill; by whom she had five children. This discrepancy, I think, can be solved, by supposing Janet having been left a young widow (Smith) and as such marrying the Fairweather. This would constitute intermarriage number four.

Alexander Don, of Ballownie, by his first wife (Elizabeth Skair) had a son Thomas, born in 1725, died in 1809, recorded on the Menmuir Monument. He married his cousin, Janet Leighton of Balrownie, constituting the second Leighton intermarriage.

The next intermarriage between Fairweathers and Dons, although not direct, occurred in 1851, when David Fairweather, in Langhaugh, married Isabella Webster, daughter of David Webster, in Mill of Balrownie, and Jean Don of Ballownie. This formed number five.

The final, or sixth, intermarriage was that of William Gerard Don (the writer) in 1889, with Jean Ann, eldest daughter of the above David in Langhaugh.

APPENDIX III.

___

Intermarriage between 'Leightons' and 'Fairweathers' in the Menmuir District.

___

N the Menmuir Register is recorded:

'4th June, 1728, Janet Leighton, spouse of the late
'John Fairweather, in Inishewan, had a lawful daughter
'Baptised, and called Elizabeth.

Inishewan is in Tannadice, but such a record occurring in
the Menmuir Session Book, shows plainly they had both
belonged originally to that parish. Very probably the widow
had returned to her relations after the death of her first husband,
and afterwards became the second wife of Alexander Don in 1731.

George Fairweather, the younger in Miltoun of Balhall, had
as his second wife Margaret Leighton, daughter of John
Leighton, Coull, Tannadice.

David Leighton, Farmer, Burnhead, Dunlappie, elder son of
David Leighton in Balrownie, had, as his first wife, Margaret
Fairweather, of the Miltoun of Balhall family.

Thomas Leighton, Brechin, (second son of David Leighton, Balrownie) married Anne Fairweather, also of the Balhall family.

Andrew Leighton, Syde, Stracathro, (third son of David Leighton, Balrownie), had, as his second wife, Janet Fairweather, his second cousin, elder daughter of Alexander Fairweather, Brechin, of the Waukmill family. This Janet's mother's maiden name was Janet Don, or Smith as a widow.

George Fairweather, Brathinch, Menmuir, (of the Kirriemuir stock), married Margaret Leighton, daughter of Thomas Leighton, Brechin.

These constitute six intermarriages.

APPENDIX IV.

Intermarriage between 'Smiths' and 'Fairweathers.'

THE descendants (if any) of the fourth person mentioned on the Menmuir Monument, 'Alexander Smith in Teagerton,' have been altogether lost sight of. The surname Smith is so common and numerous as almost to defy the tracing of relationship.

But, besides the Monument, there is a small dilapidated headstone in Menmuir churchyard, which affords some clue to the family of Alexander Smith. The part of the inscription thereon, which can be deciphered, runs as follows:

" Hier lyes Keatren fearwather who departed This life the
" 29th September, the year 1702, her Age 40 years. Some-
" time Spouse to Alexander Smith whose children were,
" Alexander, John, Ane, Isobell Smiths: heir lies Margaret
" fairweather Spouse to John Smith who died 2nd June " . .

The last pair were probably cousins, and the imperfect

inscription concerning them is evidently of a considerable later date than the first portion of the record. On the obverse are the following lines:

" Remember All. who Passeth By.

" That. Thou. Must. Die. As. Weel. as. I.

" Deaths. Sumonds; Non. Escape. It. Can.

" Remember. Therefor. Mortal. Man.

" Daylie. Thy. Sins. To. Mortifie.

" That. Thou. Mayest. Live. Eternalie."

(NOTE by the **Editor.**—The 'Keatren fearweather' here commemorated was no doubt daughter to old John in Blackhall, and her son Alexander the Smith of the Monument; thus supporting the belief that the four men mentioned thereon were at once cousins and grandsons of the said John. 'Keatren's' son John had evidently married his cousin Margaret.)

APPENDIX V.

LIST of the principal persons of the modern name Fairweather, as recorded in East Scotland previous to the last quarter of the 18th century: say from 1453 to 1779—

Robert Wedyr, Finlarg, Tealing, 1453.—James II.

Walter Fairvedder, Presbyter, Notary Public, 1547 to 1563.— Queen Mary Stuart.

Thomas Fairvedder, 1583 ⎫ Litsters or Dyers, Dundee.
Robert Fairvedder, 1609 ⎭ James VI.

John Fairvvedder, Falkland, 1591, ,, ,,

James Fawvedles or Fawvedder, 1609, Blairno, Lethnot, James VI.

Hendrie Fairvedder, Menmuir, 1609—1622 ,, ,,

John Fairvedder, Blackhall, Menmuir, 1644—1676, Charles I.-II.

Hendrie Fairvedder, Braco, Menmuir, 1644—1670, ,, ,,

John Fairvooder, Brechin, 1649 ,, ,,

Alexander ffairweather, Menmuir, 1678-1688, ,, ,,

Andrew ffairweather, 1679-1681, ,, ,,

Andrew ffairveather, Barns of Glamis, 1685, ,, ,,

William Fairweathers,
George Fairweathers, } Skippers, Dundee, 1683, Charles I-II.

Andrew Fairweather, Councillor, Brechin, 1682,   ,,   ,,

William Fairweather, junr., Skipper, Dundee, 1691, William &
Mary.

Alexander Ffairweather, junr., Bailie, Brechin, 1699-1708,
William and Mary.

Thomas Fairweather, Bailie, Dundee, 1704,   Queen Anne.

James Fairweather, Dundee, Bailie 1715, Provost 1723-33,
George II.

John Fairweather,   ,,   Bailie 1738-40,   ,,   ,,

Alexander Fairweather, Mill of Cruick,
George Fairweather, Milltoun of Ballhall, } 1717. ,,   ,,

Contemporary with, and succeeding the above, were the following Fairweathers in the Menmuir district:

James Fairweather, Mill of Brathinch, 1724.

George Fairweather, Gungeon, 1725.

John Fairweather, Inishewan, Tannadice, 1728.

Alexander Fairweather, Blairno, Lethnot, 1730.

After this date there is a blank in the Menmuir Register for a number of years, and then the following names appear:

George Fairweather, Smiddyhill, Stracathro, 1771.

Alexander Fairweather, Gairyburn, Menmuir, 1775.

Alexander Fairweather, Stracathro, 1775.

George Fairweather, Muirton, Menmuir, 1776.

David Fairweather, Halltoun or Hatton, Menmuir, 1776,

Alexander Fairweather, Balglassie, Aberlemno, 1779.

The person last named, gifted two Communion Cups to the Parish Kirk of Carraldston, of which he was probably a native.

NOTE by the Author.—The degrees of connection or relationship between these latter Fairweathers and Alexander and George of Little Cruick and Milltoun of Ballhall, cannot unfortunately be traced; but the frequency of the names Alexander and George among them points to direct relationship. The Revd. Robert Fairweather, Nigg, was descended from George, tenant in Muirtoun.

(NOTE by the Editor.—There can be no reasonable doubt, that, taking Menmuir as a centre, the Fairweathers of the surrounding parishes, Brechin, Lethnot, Careston, Aberlemno, Tannadice, Fearn, and Stracathro, were all of one blood, and not far removed in cousinship. Those farther afield, in Forfar, Glamis, Tealing, Dundee, etc., while of the same original stock, would of course, be less nearly related to the Menmuir branch.)

APPENDIX VI.

Genealogical Table (Male Line) of Fairweathers of Langhaugh

(NOTE by the Editor.—The dates affixed to the earlier ancestors are only approximate.)

1.	Hendrie Fairvedder, Blairno	-	1550—1620.
2.	John ,, ?	-	1582—1652.
3.	John ,, Blackhall	-	1610—1676.
4.	Andrew or Alexander ,,	-	1635—1700.
5.	Alexander Fairweather, Little Cruiek		1660—1719.
6.	George ,, ,, ,,		1695—1760.
7.	Alexander ,, ,, ,,		1732—1798.
8.	John ,, ,, ,, and Langhaugh		1759—1825.
9.	David ,, ,, ,,		1818—1890
10.	David ,, M.D.	-	1855—
11.	John ,, Chapelton	-	1857—

APPENDIX VII.

Genealogical Table (Male Line) Fairweathers, Mill of Balhall.

(NOTE by the Editor.—The dates affixed to earlier ancestors are only approximate).

1.	Hendrie Fairvedder, Blairno	-	1550—1620.
2.	John	,,	?	-	1582—1652.
3.	John	,,	Blackhall	-	1610—1676.
4.	Andrew or Alexander	,,	-	1635—1700.
5.	George Fairweather, Miltoun of Balhall	1672—1722.
6.	George	,,	,,	,,	1710—1770.
7.	David	,,	Balzeordie	-	1750—1810.
8.	James	,,	,, and Brechin	1788—1870.
9.	James	,,	M.D.	-	1832.
10.	James	,,
11.	Neville	,,
12.	Arthur	,,
13.	Harold	,,
14.	Ian	,,

APPENDIX VIII.

Christian Names of Fairweathers mentioned in this Book. When two or more names first only given.

MALE.		FEMALE.	
Alexander	25	Elizabeth	10
George	17	Jean, Jane	9
James	17	Margaret	7
John	16	Isobel	6
David	15	Anne	6
William	9	Agnes	6
Thomas	8	Janet	5
Robert	5	Helen	3
Andrew	4	Katherine	2
Charles	3	Magdelene	2
Hendrie	2	Mary	2
Francis	1	Jessie	1
Ludovick	1	Euphemia	1
Walter	1	Christian	1
Neville	1	Elsie	1
Arthur	1	Winifred	1
Harold	1	Aleen	1
Ian	1	Ethel	1
		Annette	1
Total	128	Total	66

APPENDIX IX.

Occupations of Fairweathers' herein mentioned.

I.	Agriculturists - - - -	42
II.	Merchants and Traders - - -	17
III.	Professional; Clerical, Law, Medicine, Military, Teachers - - -	17
IV.	Seamen - - - - -	8
V.	Undefined - - - -	42
	Total	121